"A friend is one of the nicest things you can have and one of the best things you can be."

My
Buddy Book

This Buddy Book Belongs to
A photo of me
Name:
Birthday:
My favorite color:
My hair color:
My eye color:
My favorite animal:
My favorite food:
My hobbies:

My favorite team: _______________________
When I grow up I want to be _______________________
This is how I know you: _______________________
A fun fact about me: _______________________
What I don't like: _______________________

My message or drawing for you

A photo of me

Name: _______________

Birthday: _______________

My favorite color: ⬤

My hair color: ⬤

My eye color: ⬤

My favorite animal: _______________

My favorite food: _______________

My hobbies: _______________

My favorite team: _______________________________

When I grow up I want to be _______________________________

This is how I know you: _______________________________

A fun fact about me: _______________________________

What I don't like: _______________________________

My message or drawing for you

A photo of me
Name:
Birthday:
My favorite color:
My hair color:
My eye color:
My favorite animal:
My favorite food:
My hobbies:

My favorite team: ___________________________

When I grow up I want to be ___________________________

This is how I know you: ___________________________

A fun fact about me: ___________________________

What I don't like: ___________________________

My message or drawing for you

A photo of me

Name:

Birthday:

My favorite color:

My hair color:

My eye color:

My favorite animal:

My favorite food:

My hobbies:

My favorite team: _______________________________

When I grow up I want to be _______________________________

This is how I know you: _______________________________

A fun fact about me: _______________________________

What I don't like: _______________________________

My message or drawing for you

A photo of me
Name:
Birthday:
My favorite color:
My hair color:
My eye color:
My favorite animal:
My favorite food:
My hobbies:

My favorite team: _______________________

When I grow up I want to be _______________________

This is how I know you: _______________________

A fun fact about me: _______________________

What I don't like: _______________________

My message or drawing for you

My favorite team: _______________________

When I grow up I want to be _______________________

This is how I know you: _______________________

A fun fact about me: _______________________

What I don't like: _______________________

My message or drawing for you

A photo of me
Name:
Birthday:
My favorite color:
My hair color:
My eye color:
My favorite animal:
My favorite food:
My hobbies:

My favorite team: _______________________________

When I grow up I want to be _______________________________

This is how I know you: _______________________________

A fun fact about me: _______________________________

What I don't like: _______________________________

My message or drawing for you

A photo of me
Name:
Birthday:
My favorite color:
My hair color:
My eye color:
My favorite animal:
My favorite food:
My hobbies:

My favorite team: _______________________________
When I grow up I want to be _______________________
This is how I know you: ____________________________
A fun fact about me: ______________________________
What I don't like: ________________________________

My message or drawing for you

A photo of me
Name:
Birthday:
My favorite color:
My hair color:
My eye color:
My favorite animal:
My favorite food:
My hobbies:

My favorite team: _______________________________________

When I grow up I want to be _______________________________

This is how I know you: ___________________________________

A fun fact about me: ______________________________________

What I don't like: ____

My message or drawing for you

A photo of me
Name:
Birthday:
My favorite color:
My hair color:
My eye color:
My favorite animal:
My favorite food:
My hobbies:

My favorite team: _______________________
When I grow up I want to be _______________________
This is how I know you: _______________________
A fun fact about me: _______________________
What I don't like: _______________________

My message or drawing for you

A photo of me

Name:
Birthday:
My favorite color:
My hair color:
My eye color:
My favorite animal:
My favorite food:
My hobbies:

My favorite team: ______________________________

When I grow up I want to be ______________________________

This is how I know you: ______________________________

A fun fact about me: ______________________________

What I don't like: ______________________________

My message or drawing for you

A photo of me
Name:
Birthday:
My favorite color:
My hair color:
My eye color:
My favorite animal:
My favorite food:
My hobbies:

My favorite team: _______________________________

When I grow up I want to be _______________________________

This is how I know you: _______________________________

A fun fact about me: _______________________________

What I don't like: _______________________________

My message or drawing for you

A photo of me
Name:
Birthday:
My favorite color:
My hair color:
My eye color:
My favorite animal:
My favorite food:
My hobbies:

My favorite team: _______________________________

When I grow up I want to be _______________________________

This is how I know you: _______________________________

A fun fact about me: _______________________________

What I don't like: _______________________________

My message or drawing for you

A photo of me
Name:
Birthday:
My favorite color:
My hair color:
My eye color:
My favorite animal:
My favorite food:
My hobbies:

My favorite team: _______________________________

When I grow up I want to be _______________________________

This is how I know you: _______________________________

A fun fact about me: _______________________________

What I don't like: _______________________________

My message or drawing for you

A photo of me
Name: _______________________
Birthday: _______________________
My favorite color:
My hair color:
My eye color:
My favorite animal: _______________________
My favorite food: _______________________
My hobbies: _______________________

My favorite team: _______________________________

When I grow up I want to be _______________________________

This is how I know you: _______________________________

A fun fact about me: _______________________________

What I don't like: _______________________________

My message or drawing for you

A photo of me

Name: _______________________
Birthday: _______________________
My favorite color:
My hair color:
My eye color:
My favorite animal: _______________________
My favorite food: _______________________
My hobbies: _______________________

My favorite team: _______________________________

When I grow up I want to be _______________________________

This is how I know you: _______________________________

A fun fact about me: _______________________________

What I don't like: _______________________________

My message or drawing for you

A photo of me

Name: _______________________

Birthday: _______________________

My favorite color:

My hair color:

My eye color:

My favorite animal: _______________________

My favorite food: _______________________

My hobbies: _______________________

My favorite team: ______________________________

When I grow up I want to be ______________________________

This is how I know you: ______________________________

A fun fact about me: ______________________________

What I don't like: ______________________________

My message or drawing for you

A photo of me
Name:
Birthday:
My favorite color:
My hair color:
My eye color:
My favorite animal:
My favorite food:
My hobbies:

My favorite team: _______________________________

When I grow up I want to be _______________________________

This is how I know you: _______________________________

A fun fact about me: _______________________________

What I don't like: _______________________________

My message or drawing for you

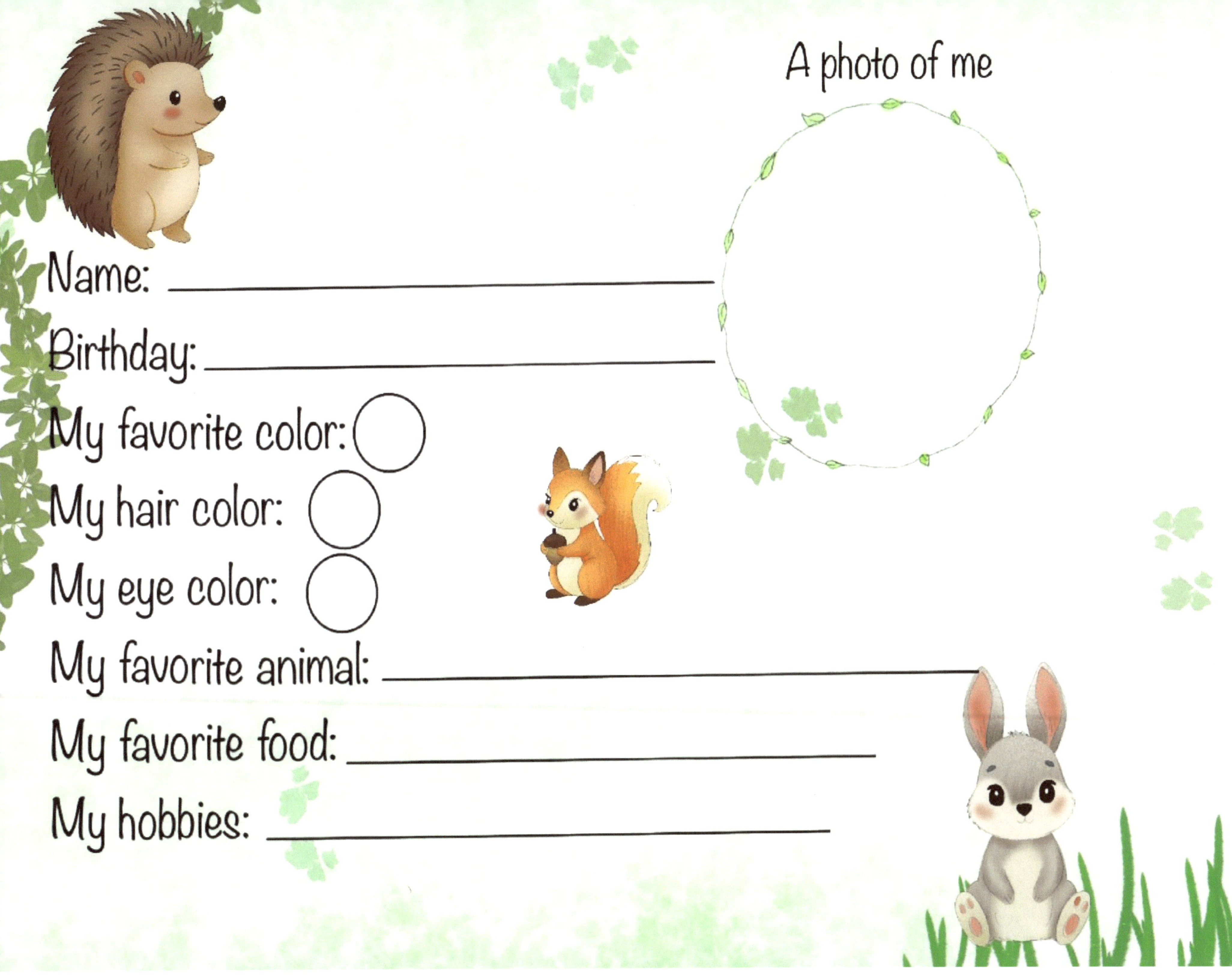

A photo of me
Name:
Birthday:
My favorite color:
My hair color:
My eye color:
My favorite animal:
My favorite food:
My hobbies:

My favorite team: _______________________________________

When I grow up I want to be _______________________________

This is how I know you: ___________________________________

A fun fact about me: _____________________________________

What I don't like: _______________________________________

My message or drawing for you

A photo of me
Name:
Birthday:
My favorite color:
My hair color:
My eye color:
My favorite animal:
My favorite food:
My hobbies:

My favorite team: _______________________________

When I grow up I want to be _______________________

This is how I know you: _______________________

A fun fact about me: _______________________

What I don't like: _______________________

My message or drawing for you

A photo of me
Name:
Birthday:
My favorite color:
My hair color:
My eye color:
My favorite animal:
My favorite food:
My hobbies:

My favorite team: ______________________________

When I grow up I want to be ______________________________

This is how I know you: ______________________________

A fun fact about me: ______________________________

What I don't like: ______________________________

My message or drawing for you

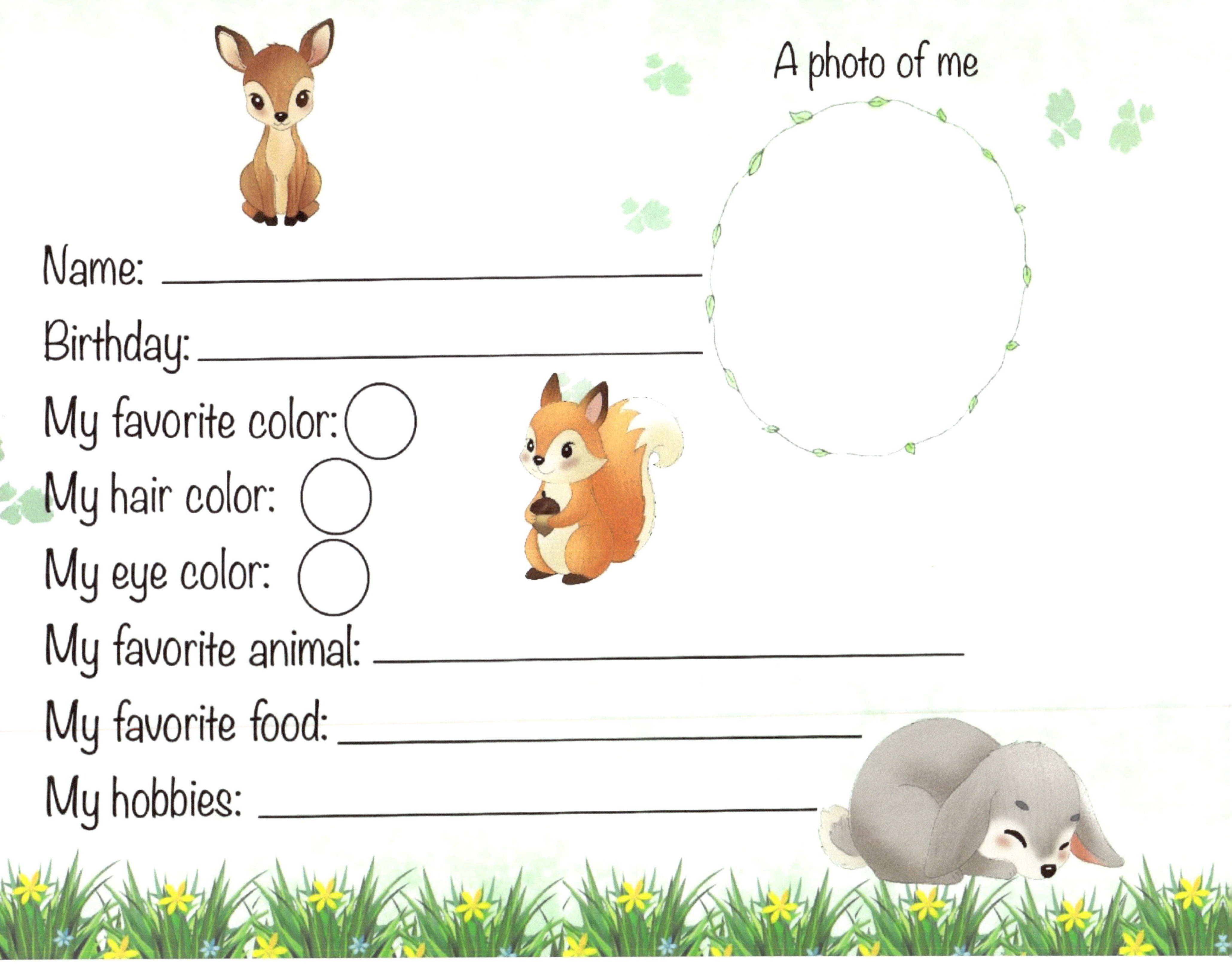

A photo of me
Name:
Birthday:
My favorite color:
My hair color:
My eye color:
My favorite animal:
My favorite food:
My hobbies:

My favorite team: _______________________________

When I grow up I want to be _______________________

This is how I know you: ___________________________

A fun fact about me: _____________________________

What I don't like: _______________________________

My message or drawing for you

A photo of me
Name: _______________________
Birthday: _____________________
My favorite color:
My hair color:
My eye color:
My favorite animal: _______________________
My favorite food: _______________________
My hobbies: _______________________

My favorite team: _______________________________

When I grow up I want to be _______________________________

A fun fact about me: _______________________________

What I don't like: _______________________________

My message or drawing for you

A photo of me

Name: _______________________

Birthday: _______________________

My favorite color:

My hair color:

My eye color:

My favorite animal: _______________________

My favorite food: _______________________

My hobbies: _______________________

My favorite team: _______________________________

When I grow up I want to be _______________________________

This is how I know you: _______________________________

A fun fact about me: _______________________________

What I don't like: _______________________________

My message or drawing for you

A photo of me

Name: _______________________

Birthday: _______________________

My favorite color:

My hair color:

My eye color:

My favorite animal: _______________________

My favorite food: _______________________

My hobbies: _______________________

My favorite team: ___________________________________

When I grow up I want to be ___________________________________

This is how I know you: ___________________________________

A fun fact about me: ___________________________________

What I don't like: ___________________________________

My message or drawing for you

A photo of me
Name: _______________________
Birthday: _______________________
My favorite color: ◯
My hair color: ◯
My eye color: ◯
My favorite animal: _______________________
My favorite food: _______________________
My hobbies: _______________________

My favorite team: _______________________
When I grow up I want to be _______________________
This is how I know you: _______________________
A fun fact about me: _______________________
What I don't like: _______________________

My message or drawing for you

A photo of me

Name: _______________________

Birthday: _______________________

My favorite color: ◯

My hair color: ◯

My eye color: ◯

My favorite animal: _______________________

My favorite food: _______________________

My hobbies: _______________________

My favorite team: _______________________________________

When I grow up I want to be _______________________________

This is how I know you: ___________________________________

A fun fact about me: _____________________________________

What I don't like: _______________________________________

My message or drawing for you

A photo of me
Name:
Birthday:
My favorite color:
My hair color:
My eye color:
My favorite animal:
My favorite food:
My hobbies:

My favorite team: ___________________________________

When I grow up I want to be ___________________________________

This is how I know you: ___________________________________

A fun fact about me: ___________________________________

What I don't like: ___________________________________

My message or drawing for you

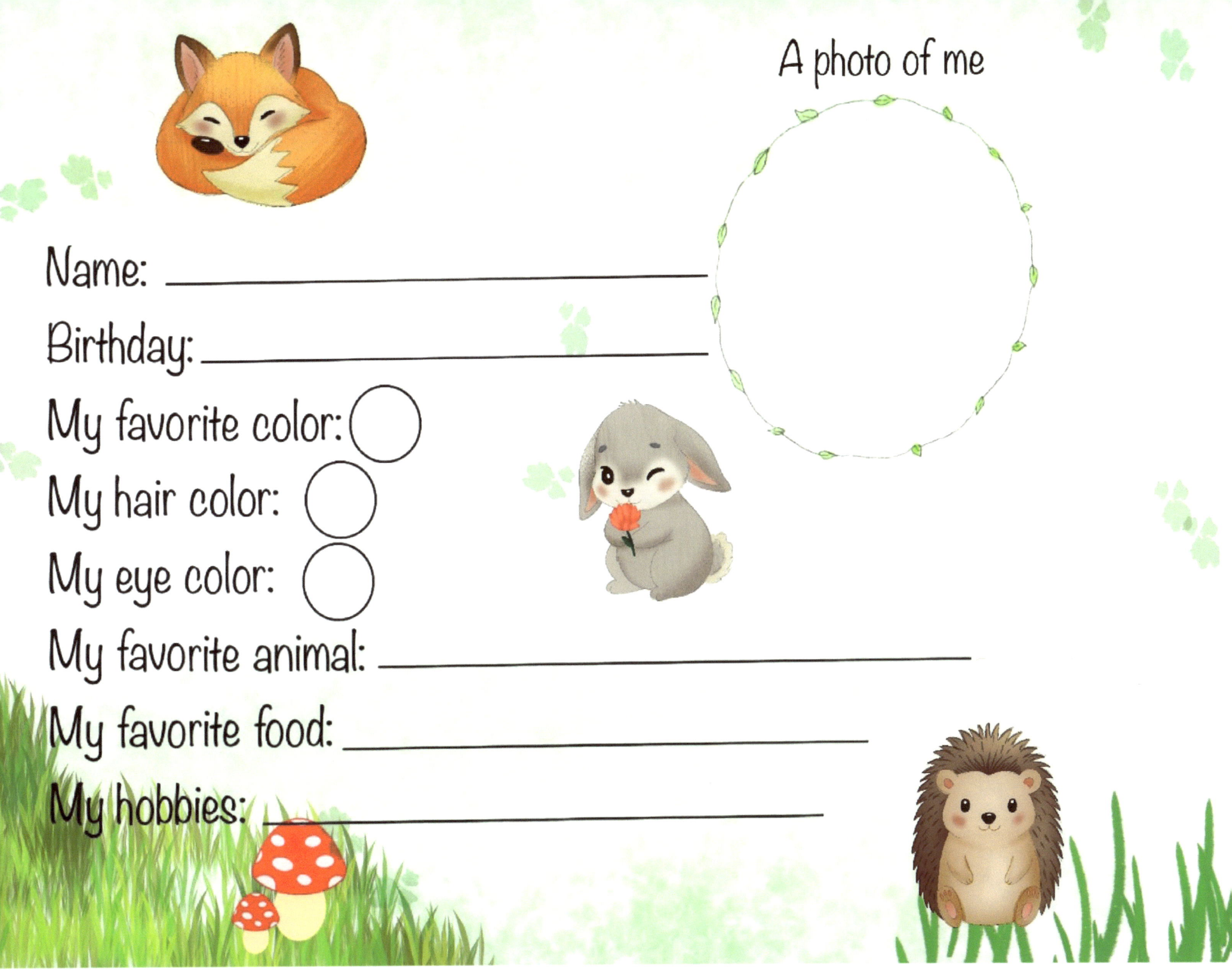A photo of me
Name:
Birthday:
My favorite color:
My hair color:
My eye color:
My favorite animal:
My favorite food:
My hobbies:

My favorite team: _______________________________

When I grow up I want to be _______________________________

This is how I know you: _______________________________

A fun fact about me: _______________________________

What I don't like: _______________________________

My message or drawing for you

A photo of me

Name: _______________________

Birthday: _______________________

My favorite color: ◯

My hair color: ◯

My eye color: ◯

My favorite animal: _______________________

My favorite food: _______________________

My hobbies: _______________________

My favorite team: _______________________

When I grow up I want to be _______________________

This is how I know you: _______________________

A fun fact about me: _______________________

What I don't like: _______________________

My message or drawing for you

A photo of me
Name:
Birthday:
My favorite color:
My hair color:
My eye color:
My favorite animal:
My favorite food:
My hobbies:

My favorite team: _______________________________

When I grow up I want to be _______________________________

This is how I know you: _______________________________

A fun fact about me: _______________________________

What I don't like: _______________________________

My message or drawing for you

A photo of me

Name: ______________________
Birthday: ______________________
My favorite color:
My hair color:
My eye color:
My favorite animal: ______________________
My favorite food: ______________________
My hobbies: ______________________

My favorite team: ___________________________

When I grow up I want to be ___________________________

This is how I know you: ___________________________

A fun fact about me: ___________________________

What I don't like: ___________________________

My message or drawing for you

A photo of me
Name:
Birthday:
My favorite color:
My hair color:
My eye color:
My favorite animal:
My favorite food:
My hobbies:

My favorite team: ______________________________

When I grow up I want to be ______________________________

This is how I know you: ______________________________

A fun fact about me: ______________________________

What I don't like: ______________________________

My message or drawing for you

A photo of me

Name: _______________________

Birthday: _______________________

My favorite color: ◯

My hair color: ◯

My eye color: ◯

My favorite animal: _______________________

My favorite food: _______________________

My hobbies: _______________________

My favorite team: _______________________

When I grow up I want to be _______________________

This is how I know you: _______________________

A fun fact about me: _______________________

What I don't like: _______________________

My message or drawing for you

A photo of me
Name:
Birthday:
My favorite color:
My hair color:
My eye color:
My favorite animal:
My favorite food:
My hobbies:

My favorite team: ______________________

When I grow up I want to be ______________________

This is how I know you: ______________________

A fun fact about me: ______________________

What I don't like: ______________________

My message or drawing for you

A photo of me
Name: _______________________
Birthday: _______________________
My favorite color: ◯
My hair color: ◯
My eye color: ◯
My favorite animal: _______________________
My favorite food: _______________________
My hobbies: _______________________

My favorite team: _________________________________

When I grow up I want to be _________________________________

This is how I know you: _________________________________

A fun fact about me: _________________________________

What I don't like: _________________________________

My message or drawing for you

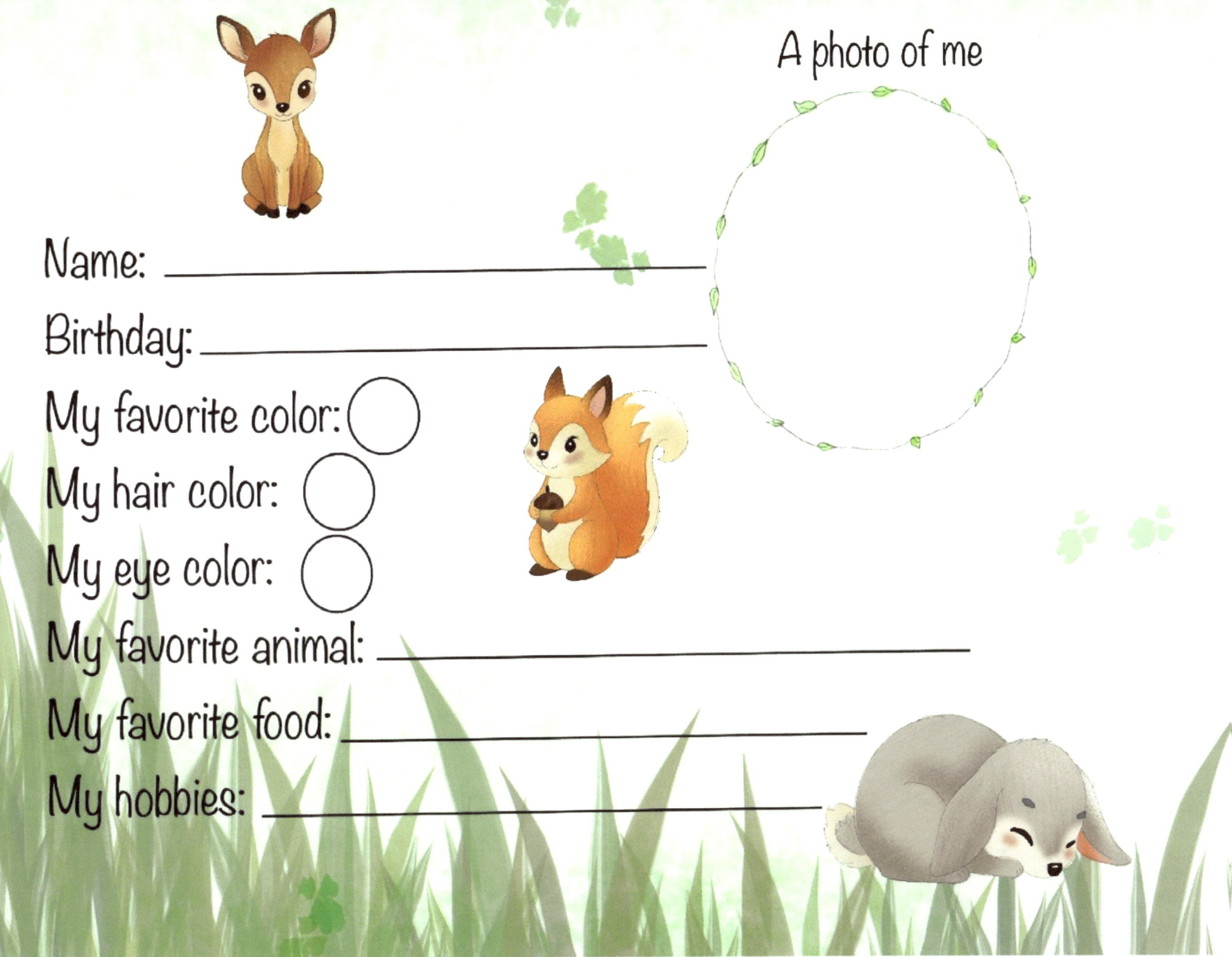

A photo of me
Name:
Birthday:
My favorite color:
My hair color:
My eye color:
My favorite animal:
My favorite food:
My hobbies:

My favorite team: ______________________________

When I grow up I want to be ______________________________

This is how I know you: ______________________________

A fun fact about me: ______________________________

What I don't like: ______________________________

My message or drawing for you

A photo of me
Name:
Birthday:
My favorite color:
My hair color:
My eye color:
My favorite animal:
My favorite food:
My hobbies:

My favorite team: _______________________________

When I grow up I want to be _______________________________

This is how I know you: _______________________________

A fun fact about me: _______________________________

What I don't like: _______________________________

My message or drawing for you

"A friend is one of
the nicest things
you can have and
one of the best
things you can be."

This charming children's friendship book invites friends to share who they are through fun, fill-in-the-blank questions and playful prompts. Each page gives kids space to write about their hobbies, favorites and personality, making it a joyful keepsake to complete, collect, and treasure. Perfect for daycare, preschool and kindergarten-age children, this book helps build connection, celebrate friendships, and create lasting memories-all while encouraging creativity and self-expression.